THE 7 CHARACTER STRENGTHS OF HIGHLY SUCCESSFUL STUDENTS ™

OPTIMISM

Huntington City
Township Public Library
255 West Park Drive
Huntington, IN 46750

TERRY TEAGUE MEYER

rosen publishing's
rosen
central

NEW YORK

Published in 2014 by The Rosen Publishing Group, Inc.
29 East 21st Street, New York, NY 10010

Library of Congress Cataloging-in-Publication Data

Meyer, Terry Teague.
Optimism/by Terry Teague Meyer.—1st ed.—New York: Rosen, © 2014
      p. cm.—(The 7 character strengths of highly successful students)
Includes bibliographical references and index.
ISBN: 978-1-4488-9545-8 (library binding)
ISBN: 978-1-4488-9561-8 (paperback)
ISBN: 978-1-4488-9562-5 (6-pack)
1. Optimism—Juvenile literature. 2. Optimism. 3. Positive psychology.
4. Success—Psychological aspects. I. Title.
BF575.O67 .M49 2014
149.5

Manufactured in the United States of America

CPSIA Compliance Information: Batch #S13YA: For further information, contact Rosen Publishing, New York, New York, at 1-800-237-9932.

CONTENTS

INTRODUCTION

elevision stations all around the United States reported on Dawn Loggins's graduation from high school in Lawndale, North Carolina, in the spring of 2012. A straight-A student, Dawn was the first in her town to be headed to Harvard—on a full-tuition scholarship. But what made the national media and millions of Americans take note was the fact that Dawn's parents had abandoned her before her senior year. The young woman had to work as a school janitor in order to support herself.

Despite her personal problems, Dawn kept up her grades, held leadership positions in her school, and, all by herself, dealt with the complicated process of applying to colleges. Graduating from high school and getting a scholarship to a top university is a challenge for any student. How did someone with so many obstacles to overcome succeed in spite of all that could have held her back?

Psychologists (scientists who study the human mind and human behavior) also wonder why some individuals succeed in situations so difficult that most people fail

Optimism and community support carried Dawn Loggins from poverty and homelessness to a bright future as a Harvard student.

or give up trying. Scientific studies have shown that certain personal qualities lead to success in life. Fortunately, someone doesn't have to be born with these qualities. Anyone can learn and develop them through practice. Optimism, a sense of hopefulness and confidence about the future, is one of these key characteristics.

In the case of Dawn Loggins, her positive attitude helped her see beyond the poverty and abandonment that characterized her childhood. Instead, she looked ahead to the college education that would help her create a better life. When her parents abandoned her, she didn't tell herself that it was her fault. She had confidence in her intelligence and looked for support among teachers and administrators at her school. Having overcome many disadvantages to become an outstanding student, she could visualize herself meeting the challenges of college. Rather than assume a university as competitive as Harvard would not accept her, she aimed high and was rewarded for her belief in herself and her hard work. Dawn expressed her optimism when she told Vivian Kuo of Cable News Network (CNN), "I know my future is going to be great."

Once her story was publicized, Dawn received well-wishes and donations from people all around the world. She hopes to use this money to start a nonprofit to help other needy teens in her area. Optimism helps individuals do great things and seems to have a positive ripple effect. Once optimistic people get past the obstacles in their lives and reach their personal goals, they tend to want to help others. And most optimists do not merely think about helping others. They take direct and concrete action to do whatever is needed to make it happen.

Studies show the benefits of an optimistic approach to life. Some people are born optimists. But an optimistic attitude can also be learned and become a habit. Some schools have begun teaching optimism and other positive character strengths along with subjects like math and language arts. What is optimism? How does someone become more optimistic? And what good things can result from making a positive attitude a habit? The answers lie just ahead.

CHAPTER 1

OPTIMISM AND ITS OPPOSITE

The word "optimism" comes from the Latin word for "best thing." It describes an attitude—a way of thinking—of expecting most situations to turn out well. The opposite of optimism is pessimism. The difference between these two attitudes or habits of mind is often illustrated by the way someone would describe a glass filled midway to the top. The optimist's view is that the glass is half full; it is on its way to becoming complete.

Optimists view life with a positive attitude. Many people are born optimists, but others can learn optimism and make it a habit.

The pessimist would describe the same glass as half empty; its water will soon be used up.

When we talk about whether someone is optimistic or pessimistic, we are describing a personality trait, not just a way of seeing a given situation. A trait is something that distinguishes one person from another. Brown eyes, curly hair, or a round face are physical traits. What we call personality is a combination of nonphysical traits that make a person unique (unlike anyone else). Let's say that Sally is shy around strangers, she loves dogs, she's always on time, and she prefers outdoor activities to playing video games. All of these and many other habits, behaviors, and attitudes make Sally different from her family, friends, or anyone else. If Sally is an optimist, she most often sees situations in a positive light. Even if things go wrong, she doesn't expect a bad situation to be permanent.

IT'S ALL HOW YOU LOOK AT IT

An optimist (someone with a positive outlook) and a pessimist (someone with a negative outlook) would typically view the same situations differently. Because they don't see things the same way, they behave and react differently. These differences in behavior, in turn, affect their relationships with others and the directions their lives take.

Optimism can give someone the confidence to try out for activities, like a team sport. But the individual's success in any area also requires hard work, dedication, and practice.

Consider how an optimist and a pessimist would view typical school situations. When trying out for a sports team, a role in the school play, or to be ranked in a school band, the optimistic student expects to be successful. The optimist's attitude promotes success by providing the confidence to help him or her perform well. An extreme pessimist might not even show up for tryouts. He or she would not expect to be chosen and might want to avoid the pain of being rejected. Expecting failure is a bad way to prepare for success. When taking a test, the optimist has the advantage of being more confident about the outcome. The pessimist is more likely to be nervous and less able to recall what was learned.

Being optimistic does not equal being unrealistic. Optimism encourages people to take risks, but not foolish ones. Even the most optimistic person would not cross a busy street against the light, expecting all to turn out well. The beginning musician would not expect to be chosen for the top school band. An athlete with a physical disadvantage must realize that making the team will require him or her to work harder than everyone else.

OPTIMISM IS GOOD FOR YOU

The many benefits of being optimistic offer good reasons to have a positive attitude. Consider days when you're in a good mood or a bad mood. Which do you prefer? Optimism is related to a sense of hope about the future and cheerfulness in the present, and that just feels good. So a sense of optimism is rewarding in itself. But there are other benefits as well. Optimists are more attractive to others in social situations. Think about it. Are you more likely to be drawn to someone who has a sunny outlook or someone who looks worried, defeated, or sour? People who expect things to turn out well are more likely to be open to meeting new people. They don't expect to be rejected.

People with a sunny outlook on life are naturally more attractive to their peers. As a result, they enjoy a more active social life.

Being optimistic feels good, makes people more socially attractive, and also helps them live longer. As reported in the *New York Times*, a Harvard University study of eight thousand people showed a lower incidence of heart disease among those who reported more happiness or satisfaction in certain key areas of their lives, such as work and family. The researchers concluded that traits like optimism and hope were linked to reduced risk of heart disease and stroke. Prior to this study, scientists had already shown that depression and anxiety could worsen the outcomes for such patients.

Tali Sharot, an expert on psychology and brain science, reports on a different study that indicates that optimists are likely to live longer than pessimists. This report tracked one thousand people over a period of fifty years and found pessimists more likely to die from accidental or violent deaths. The study concluded that pessimists were more likely to engage in risky behaviors because they felt that they didn't have much to lose. Optimists, Sharot says, are more selective about taking risks. Because they envision a good life ahead, they are less likely to engage in any activity—like smoking—that is likely to cut that good life short.

Given all of this evidence that optimism makes for a long, healthy, and happy life, why would anyone be a pessimist? Pessimism comes naturally to many people. Problems such as illness, having to move away from friends, the death of a loved one, or a parent losing a job can lead to a negative outlook on life in general. This negative outlook can then become a reflex, a habit of mind, a worldview. Yet some people, like Dawn Loggins, remain optimistic in spite of great difficulties. Why do some people pick themselves up and start over when life knocks them down, while others become discouraged? Optimism is a character strength that helps individuals survive and overcome bad situations.

The good news for natural pessimists is that they can learn to become more optimistic.

OPTIMISM IN ACTION

Many people see optimism as an example of a self-fulfilling prophecy. A prophecy is a prediction of what will happen in the future. A self-fulfilling prophecy is a prediction that comes true just because someone said it would and believed it would. The idea might seem strange, but it points to the relationship between belief and action. A young person who predicts that he or she will become a spelling champion will have to study a lot of words to make that prediction come true. But having made the prediction, he or she is already aiming for success and committing him- or herself to the hard work necessary to make it come true.

There is an important relationship between optimism and action. Psychologist Suzanne Segerstrom has conducted a great deal of research in this area and concluded, "Having optimistic beliefs gets you only so far. You have to get the rest of the way through doing." In other words, just sitting around thinking happy thoughts is not what makes optimists successful. It is how an optimistic attitude inspires them to act that makes all the difference. Professional basketball has featured some short players in the past—like Tyrone Bogues (5'3" [160 centimeters]) and NBA Hall of Fame member Calvin Murphy (5'9" [175 cm]). They didn't assume it was useless to try out for the team. They worked so hard that they excelled despite physical disadvantages in their chosen sport.

How exactly is optimism related to action? Basically, the more someone believes that a positive outcome can be achieved in a situation, the harder that person is likely to work toward that outcome. And the harder someone works, the more likely he or she is to reach a goal. People who expect to do well on a test know that they have to understand and master the information upon which they will be tested. By studying, doing homework, and maybe even going for tutoring, students who expect to do well make sure that they do in fact perform well.

Tyrone "Mugsy" Bogues found success as a professional basketball player in spite of being shorter than the average player. His optimism and determination helped him overcome a physical disadvantage.

ARE YOU AN OPTIMIST OR A PESSIMIST?

Take this quiz to help you determine if you are an optimist or a pessimist:

How would you likely react in the following situations?

1. YOU LEFT A FEW ANSWERS BLANK ON A TEST.
   a. You figure you'll pass anyway.
   b. You're sure you'll fail.
   c. You ask the teacher for tutoring.

2. YOUR BEST FRIEND IS MOVING TO ANOTHER SCHOOL.
   a. You know you'll keep in touch one way or another.
   b. You're never going to be able to replace him/her.
   c. You start planning a going-away party.

3. YOUR BOYFRIEND/GIRLFRIEND DUMPS YOU.
   a. You decide you really didn't care for him/her that much.
   b. You stay in your room for a week and eat lots of junk food and are convinced you'll never fall in love again.
   c. You decide to channel your emotions in a positive direction and sign up for a walk for charity.

4. YOU SEE A SCHOOL PRESENTATION ABOUT THE DANGERS OF CLIMATE CHANGE.

a. You don't pay any attention because you know there's another side to the story.

b. You talk to your parents about moving to northern Canada.

c. You talk to your science teacher to get more information.

5. YOU DIDN'T MAKE THE CUT TO BE ON THE VOLLEYBALL TEAM.

a. You figure all the other players were taller.

b. You decide to give up on sports.

c. You decide to keep practicing and wait for next year.

If you answered mostly "b," you are clearly a pessimist. The "a" and "c" answers show a positive attitude. Yet the "a" answers indicate a positive though passive attitude. The positivity leads to acceptance of a situation but doesn't get translated into equally productive action. In contrast, the "c" answers show a willingness to take positive action in a given situation that will lead to improved circumstances, greater understanding and clarity, or improved chances of future success. Taking an active role in life is typical of optimists.

Optimism creates a kind of upward spiral to success. Success and recognition make people feel good and motivates them as well. Take a young artist whose drawing is accepted in a school-wide competition.

Even if the work doesn't win a prize, being recognized will make the artist want to draw more. Earning a ribbon provides even more incentive to keep making art, to improve, and to pick up new skills and techniques.

Of course, life doesn't always go the way we'd like. Obstacles big and small present challenges to success. But the optimist will see roadblocks for what they are—things one must work to overcome or adapt to. The pessimist may see only more problems and failures ahead and consider a roadblock to be insurmountable, the end of the road. He or she will give up and turn around without even trying to get past the roadblock.

OVERCOMING "LEARNED HELPLESSNESS"

Optimists don't just assume things will turn out well. They also work to improve the chances for positive outcomes. On the other hand, a pessimistic attitude is related to what one psychologist terms "learned helplessness." Studies on lab rats have shown that when test animals learn that they can't control what happens to them, they give up trying. Lab animals can be trained to push buttons or perform other activities either to get rewards (food) or avoid pain (like a mild shock). But when rewards or punishment seems random and unrelated to what they do, animals often stop making any effort. Instead of learning how to do something to get a reward, the test animals become trained to give up and do nothing.

The behavior of lab animals who have given up appears similar to that of humans when they are depressed. Depression is a mental state in which a person feels so sad that he or she withdraws from normal daily life. Extremely depressed people may have difficulty sleeping and may show no interest in the most basic activities, like eating. It is easy to see how depression and "learned helplessness" are related to pessimism.

Young people experiencing difficulties and setbacks should actively seek out the help of teachers, counselors, and coaches.

Someone who is already sad is unlikely to see the positive side of things. Without a sense of hope, someone might give up making any effort to improve a situation. He or she might assume that things will turn out badly no matter what—so why bother trying?

Optimists, on the other hand, don't see a negative situation as something that can't change. They might wait and see if the situation improves. Often it does. The bad weather passes. The unemployed parent gets a job. The broken leg mends. A more active approach (often called "proactive") is even more effective. The student who asks for tutoring is bound to do better on the next test—even if he or she didn't fail the last one. Planning a going-away party for a good friend is a way to honor the friendship, take one's mind off the sadness of parting, and meet new friends or get to know others better. Such responses to challenges, obstacles, and stumbling blocks perfectly illustrate the popular saying: "If life gives you lemons, make lemonade!"

CHAPTER 2

TALKING TO YOURSELF

Whether someone is an optimist or a pessimist depends a great deal on how the individual reacts to situations. While the optimist is more likely to act in response to a difficult or challenging situation, the pessimist is more likely to do little or nothing. Choosing action or inaction is largely a consequence of how the individual thinks about the situation.

People are always talking to themselves in their thoughts. Sometimes we are very aware of our thoughts; often we don't pay much attention. Even when we are largely unaware of our thoughts, however, they still affect how we act or react throughout our daily lives. A certain way of talking to oneself can become a habit and, in this way, can become a firmly fixed part of who someone is. One of these self-talk habits is what psychologists call "explanatory style." This is the way that someone mentally explains the reasons for situations and events that occur in his or her life.

The way someone thinks about a situation—with positive or negative thoughts—can have a tremendous influence on its outcome. Positive thoughts are more likely to lead to positive actions and outcomes.

When talking about physical and character traits earlier, it was noted that we are born with certain characteristics. Some physical traits, like skin and eye color, cannot be changed. Others, like height, change as children grow and people age. However, it is possible to change your weight and body composition (amount of muscle) through diet, exercise, and self-control. Just as someone can lose weight and build strength by developing good eating and exercise habits, one can build new mental habits and develop positive character traits through attention and practice.

A CHALLENGE TO OVERCOME OR AN IMPASSABLE ROADBLOCK?

Everyone has problems they must deal with. In their minds, optimists tend to explain or characterize setbacks and disappointments as temporary. They consider failures as one-time mistakes. They see an obstacle as something to overcome, a mere bump in the road. The pessimist, on the other hand, is likely to consider an obstacle to be overwhelming, insurmountable, wearying rather than energizing, and a sign of more bad things to come. Pessimists tend to regard personal mistakes as a sign of weakness or as a basic character flaw that will create problems for them in other areas of their lives.

Consider some typical situations in the life of a young person. Pessimistic Pete fails an English test. He starts thinking: "I hate English. I'm no good at it. I'll probably get an F. I'm not so good at history either. School is so hard for me. I must be stupid. My parents want me to go to college, but how can I if I mess up in middle school? I'm always disappointing my parents , and I will always be a failure." Olivia the optimist, who failed the same English test, tells herself that she should simply have studied more for it.

A single bad grade or disappointment doesn't mean more bad things are ahead, but pessimists tend to think this is true. Optimists are more likely to see a failure as a one-time setback, a temporary situation, and call to action.

She doesn't see a setback like failing one test as the permanent, definitive, and conclusive mark of being a bad student. Pete's train of thought might seem a little extreme, but disappointments can easily lead someone to start mentally beating himself or herself up.

In the case of a failed test (or even a failed class), the individual can take responsibility for the results by, for

The first and second place women's wheelchair competitors race to the finish in the Boston Marathon. An optimistic outlook helps physically challenged people adapt and thrive.

example, studying harder and getting tutoring help. Often obstacles and setbacks come at random, however, without warning and through no fault of the individual. Illness or disability strikes some people and spares others, but how the person views the situation is very important.

THE AUTHOR'S OWN STORY

I have always been an optimist. I experienced ups and downs like everyone else, but I felt generally lucky about my life. In 2003, I found a lump in my breast (which had not shown up on a recent mammogram), but I felt sure it was not a serious risk. However, as a realistic optimist, I had a biopsy.

When the doctor told me I had a cancerous tumor, my first thought was that I was going to die. So much for a positive attitude. Surgery to remove the tumor showed that the cancer had spread to a lymph node, meaning I would need to undergo chemotherapy as well as radiation. Unsure how I would react to chemotherapy, I said good-bye to my high school students, not knowing if I would return to teach them the next week or if I would be forced to miss the rest of the school year.

I tolerated the chemo very well and was able to teach throughout my treatments. I was overwhelmed when I returned to school by the outpouring of support and personal stories from my students and their families. Through them, I discovered how many mothers, grandmothers, aunts, and sisters had recovered from breast cancer. As a result, my attitude shifted, and I began to see my treatments as a long, slow path that would lead exactly where I wanted to go—toward a return to good health. I thought of my experience in treatment as akin to being pregnant—a process requiring many trips to the doctor but that would finally end in a positive and joyous outcome.

During treatment, I experienced many feelings of helplessness. At one point, I met with a counselor and confessed that I believed I would never be truly healthy again. She disputed this belief and carefully pointed out that there was no actual reason to believe it. She was right. Ten years later, I am cancer-free and in better health than before the diagnosis.

It would be untrue to say that an optimistic attitude led to my overcoming cancer. I credit the care and expertise of the many health care professionals who helped me recover. However, I know that my positive attitude helped me through what was an extremely unpleasant experience. Had I not believed I would recover, I would not have been able to lead a somewhat normal life during the treatment. My family, friends, and students would have also had to deal with my moping, and we all would have suffered more.

Imagine suddenly learning you will be confined to a wheelchair for life. Then imagine the difference in your quality of life if you told yourself that you were now a worthless person and could never be happy. What if instead, you kept reminding yourself that you were basically the same person you were before the illness or disability struck, and that many, many people lead full and happy lives in wheelchairs? You would be well on your way to becoming one of those people who lead rich and fulfilling lives, enlivened and illuminated by optimism and positivity.

CHANGE THE WAY YOU THINK

Dawn Loggins and Jesse Jean, a young man whose story was told over the years on National Public Radio (NPR), are examples of young people with positive explanatory styles.

Dawn never told herself that she deserved to grow up in poverty or caused her parents to abandon her. Jesse Jean, whose father was sent to jail after murdering Jesse's mother, grew up in an area infested by gangs and crime. His background and surroundings made his future look dismal. But instead of giving up, he sought out mentors at his neighborhood teen center. They helped him graduate from high school and college. He was told as a child that he would never amount to anything. His reaction? "Me being the person I am, it motivated me."

Setbacks can motivate people to adapt to new situations and find creative solutions to overcome any and all obstacles to their success.

As psychologist Elaine Fox writes, "The important thing is having a sense of control over your life, your destiny. When you have a setback, you feel you can do something about it." Changing one's thoughts is not easy. You must first pay attention to your thoughts and view them objectively. Objectively means examining something in a detached way, without emotion. That's not easy either, but distancing yourself from negative thoughts is a first step to becoming more positive.

Act like a scientist and consider which thoughts make sense. It might be helpful to consider how you would advise a friend in the same situation. Oddly, people are often harder on themselves than they would ever be on someone else. If a good friend's parent lost a job and the family had to make sacrifices, you would not say things like: "All your friends are going to look down on you now." "You won't be able to have any fun." Such cruel statements are also very exaggerated. Yet when someone's own thoughts lead in such a negative direction, he or she is unlikely to question whether the thinking is realistic or exaggerated, accurate or erroneous, and whether the fear is justified or irrational.

CHAPTER 3

LEARNING OPTIMISM

Optimism is a character strength that can be learned and developed through practice. There are a number of steps a pessimist can take to develop a more positive attitude. Changing one's outlook on life requires one to use objectivity, imagination, and persistence. What are these traits? How does one use them as learning tools to become more optimistic?

STEP BACK AND BE OBJECTIVE

Someone who is objective looks clearly at situations without any distorted coloring of his or her personal feelings and emotions. The opposite of objective is subjective. A subjective viewpoint is colored by a person's opinions or feelings.

Consider how objectivity could lead to improving a negative situation. Jean, who lives with her father and his new wife, resents having to share her room with her younger stepsister, Olivia, on weekends. Her father and

Using objectivity to see things from other people's points of view fosters family harmony. Open family communication and flexibility are also important.

stepmother don't seem to understand what a hardship it is to have a little girl invading Jean's private space. Consequently, Jean has started wondering if her father loves her as much as he used to, now that he has a new wife and stepdaughter. She finds it hard to be nice to Olivia and feels her father and stepmother always side with the younger girl. Jean has a pessimistic explanatory style. Her thoughts are telling her that she's not a nice person and that she's selfish and unlovable.

She also thinks that Olivia is a brat, and she doubts that they will ever get along.

Jean talks about the situation with a school counselor and then her father. She starts to view the situation more objectively, and things begin to look up. She is reminded that no one means to punish her by making her share her room; there is simply no other place for Olivia to stay. Once she considers the problem more objectively, Jean starts working to improve the situation by discussing with Olivia and her parents how best to share the bedroom space while maintaining a sense of privacy. Focusing on how to deal with the obstacle at hand, Jean starts feeling better about herself and her stepsister. She can now envision them becoming closer in the future.

USE YOUR IMAGINATION

The human imagination allows people to feel they have experienced things they have not actually experienced. In daydreams, we can visit faraway places and meet famous people, both living and dead. The imagination can also enable an optimist to foresee a successful future in great detail.

Several neuroscientists conducted experiments in which they asked volunteers to imagine events that might occur during the next five years. Some of these events were positive, like winning a large sum of money or going out on an enjoyable date. Other events were negative, like losing a wallet or ending a romantic relationship. Magnetic resonance scanners recorded the brain activity of the subjects while they imagined the future. Most subjects reported that their images of good events were more detailed and vivid, while the negative and unwanted events seemed more blurry. When subjects imagined positive events, their brain scans showed more activity in the parts of the brain responsible for processing emotions and motivation. Other research has shown that people who are very depressed have difficulty creating detailed images of future events.

The American women's gymnastics team won big at the 2012 Olympics. The team members' visions of success began in childhood and motivated them through years of practice and training.

Brain scans of depressed people show communication problems in those same parts of the brain.

The imagination can provide bright pictures of the future you want and even help you plan how to achieve that future. However, the imagination can also be a source of worry. If your parent is late to pick you up, you might imagine the reason is a car crash or some other accident. The pessimist might wonder if an upset stomach is food poisoning or a dreaded disease recently featured in the news.

You can control your imagination, but it's a little like a puppy that runs off in all directions. Put it on a leash, and the master controls where it goes. Controlling your imagination and sending it in a positive direction requires awareness of the power of thought. A common stress-reduction technique involves clearing the mind of negative thoughts by actively promoting pleasant thoughts. In such mental exercises, people are guided by a teacher or group leader to imagine being at a beach or other relaxing place. In order to become fully immersed in the scene, they are then instructed to imagine the sights, sounds, and smells of that place further. Heart rates go down, stress drains away, and a positive outlook emerges.

Olympic athletes are examples of people who use imagination and hard work to achieve their goals. A sense of optimism is part of what keeps every Olympic athlete working toward his or her goal. Knowing that everyone

CAINE'S ARCADE

The story of Caine Monroy and his cardboard arcade shows how far imagination and optimism can take someone. One summer, nine-year-old Caine spent every day with his father at his car parts store. Caine, who loved to build things and loved arcade games, began building games out of cardboard boxes. His arcade soon filled the empty storefront, and Caine prepared for customers to stop in and play games. He wore a T-shirt printed "Caine's Arcade" and readied tickets and prizes, but no one came in (there were few pedestrians in the area).

When school resumed in the fall, Caine kept the arcade open on the weekends—still without any customers. Finally, Nirvan Mullick, a filmmaker, stopped in for a car part and recognized how clever the arcade was. He bought a "fun pass" and kept coming back. When Mullick learned that he was Caine's only customer, he decided that more people should know about the arcade. He made a short film about Caine and secretly planned to bring hundreds of people to the arcade on Caine's birthday. When Nirvan's film appeared on YouTube, Caine's Arcade quickly became a worldwide sensation.

can't be a winner, or even qualify to compete, the young athlete must be able to imagine herself or himself in the winner's place of honor.

A CNN interview with the 2012 American women's gymnastics team, known as the Fierce Five, highlights the positive attitude of the young women who shared a team gold medal and earned numerous individual medals as well.

Gabby Douglas, the women's all-around gold medalist, said that she felt confident going into the competition because she had worked for so many years. Jordyn Wieber was disqualified from the individual all-around competition. But she credited her ability to perform well in the later team competition to looking forward to the next phase of the games and her desire to help lead her team to the gold medal podium.

DISTRACT YOURSELF

One way to avoid sinking into a swamp of negative thoughts is through distraction. Distraction is something that turns someone's attention from his or her current focus to something else. For example, while watching television, someone could be distracted by a person walking in front of the screen. While doing homework, you might be distracted by a text from a friend. Intentional distraction can help chase away negative thoughts. Rather than dwell on the negative (Why wasn't I invited to that party? Am I not good enough? Will I ever be popular?), choose instead to think of something else. This might be an upcoming soccer game or trip to the mall, for example. For distraction to work, it's essential to recognize when your thoughts are taking you in a bad direction.

QUESTION THE FACTS

Another way to deal with thoughts that lead to a sense of helplessness is to challenge and dispute them. To dispute something is to question whether or not it is true, just as a lawyer might challenge a witness in a courtroom. Someone having trouble making friends or fitting in at school might feel doomed to lifelong loneliness. But a friend, parent, or counselor could argue rightly that this just isn't so. You could also have a debate with yourself and come up with arguments to counter pessimistic thoughts.

MAKE COMPARISONS

People often compare themselves to others, sometimes without even being aware of it. Making deliberate comparisons can be helpful in promoting optimism and a sense of control over your life. Oddly, it can work whether you compare yourself favorably or unfavorably to someone else. People who have accomplished something outstanding can inspire others to do the same. A writer often makes his or her readers want to become writers as well. Watching the achievements of Olympic athletes inspires young viewers to take up sports or train harder. Many medal winners have credited the sight of a former champion receiving an award as inspiration for the belief that they could do the same.

On the other hand, comparing yourself to someone who has not accomplished as much as you have can help you appreciate who you are and where you are at on the road toward your goal. The disappointed student who didn't get a leading role in the school pageant might think about those who didn't make it past the first round of tryouts.

Beyoncé and Tina Turner in a duet at the Grammy Awards. Successful people serve as role models to young people, inspiring them to believe they also can achieve greatness. Turner inspired Beyoncé when she was a young girl, and now Beyoncé is inspiring the next generation of young people who cherish dreams of success.

You may not have earned a medal in a race, but it may help to consider how many runners crossed the finish line after you. Of course, you should keep these comparisons private to avoid making someone else feel bad about his or her performance.

OPTIMISM IN SCHOOLS

Techniques to improve optimism are now being taught in schools. This movement for positive education aims to increase students' happiness while they gain knowledge. The purpose of the movement is to promote learning and prevent depression among young people. The University of Pennsylvania has developed the Penn Resiliency Program to promote optimism by teaching students to think more realistically and flexibly about their problems. A two-year program for ninth-graders has resulted in improved grades and behavior. Plus, students ended up liking school more.

One of the exercises in the program calls for students to write about three good things that happened to them that day. They would do this every day, for a week. The things could be important or not so important ("I answered a really hard question correctly in language arts today.") Students also write why they think each good thing happened and what they could do to bring about more good things in the future. In this way, students learned to notice positive things in their lives, to consider how they occurred or were brought about, and to become more active in bringing about other positive outcomes.

Students at the KIPP Delta College Preparatory School in Arkansas are trained in character strengths at the same time as they are taught their academic subjects.

As reported by educational writer Paul Tough, schools like the prestigious Riverdale Country School in New York and the nationwide network of KIPP (Knowledge Is Power Preparatory) academies have made teaching optimism and other character strengths a part of their instructional program. These schools encourage teachers to include discussions of character strengths, such as optimism and persistence, as they also teach reading, social studies, and other subjects. The schools issue "character growth cards" from time to time, which rate a student's level of achievement in these areas. The educators at these schools recognize that mastering academic subjects is not the only measure of a student's success.

David Levin is the cofounder of the KIPP program. He became interested in the importance of character development when he noticed that students from disadvantaged backgrounds who had made great strides at KIPP schools were having more trouble than expected once they got into college. After doing some research, the educators realized that grades and scores on the Scholastic Aptitude Test (SAT) didn't accurately predict who would be most successful in college. Character strengths, like optimism, were more accurate and important predictors of academic success in college.

Teaching children how to add, subtract, multiply, and divide has been going on for years. Teaching them character strengths such as optimism and self-control presented a new challenge to the educators. However, once they recognized these character strengths as habits rather than in-born traits, they began to make them an important part of their school program.

From the start, KIPP schools used slogans, banners, and T-shirts to keep students focused on their goal of both academic and character-based success. Students were encouraged to fill out and post a "Spotted" card when they noticed a fellow student demonstrating a particular character strength. These character strengths are posted in classrooms, included in many class discussions, and almost always come up in discussions about behavior problems.

Tom Brunzell is the dean of students at KIPP Infinity (a middle school). He sees the KIPP program as a way to help students use their conscious minds to understand and overcome unconscious fears and bad habits. According to Brunzell, "The kids who make it are the ones who can tell themselves, 'I can rise above this little situation. I'm OK. Tomorrow is a new day.'"

CHAPTER 4

SPREADING OPTIMISM

Many young people whose optimism has helped them overcome serious obstacles have gone on to share the rewards of their success with others. Perhaps because they are confident that more good things will come their way, they are generous and want to help others. Dawn Loggins plans to help other homeless students. Jesse Jean, who survived childhood in a neighborhood full of gangs and drugs, mentored other young people while he was in college.

Filmmaker Nirvan Mullick *(far left)* made a film about Caine Monroy *(second from left)* that resulted in the creation of a foundation and competitions to inspire creativity in young people around the world.

STAY ON THE SUNNY SIDE

Quick pointers to help you stay on the sunny side of the street:

- **Don't claim the blame:** Everything bad that happens to you isn't your fault. Even when you know you've made a mistake, it doesn't mean there's anything wrong with you.
- **Get ready for action:** Mistakes, setbacks, and plain old bad luck are all obstacles that you may be able to overcome. Consider problems objectively, and make a plan to get around them. Then follow through with the plan.
- **Tomorrow is another day:** Sometimes a situation that seems hopeless improves over time. It may improve by itself or you may simply change your attitude. A new day may mean a new outlook on a situation. Give it some time.
- **Adapt:** Your behavior and thinking are really the only things you can control. You may not like a situation, but you can be flexible and adapt.
- **Notice anything good lately?** Make a habit of noticing the good things in your life. You might want to keep a journal of things you can be grateful for. This will also provide good reading for days when things aren't going well. You might be surprised at how many good things there are going on in your life once you take the time to make an accounting.

The willingness of these young optimists to help others is not surprising. People who have overcome obstacles are likely to want to share their success with others in the same situation. Their ability to see beyond the problems of the present and envision a brighter future for themselves enables them to imagine similar positive outcomes for others. Also, these young people were able to form a plan of action and carry it out. Sometime these actions were small ones, like working hard in school or asking for extra help. But the positive results of these first steps led to successes and actions with even bigger results.

OPTIMISTS PAY IT FORWARD

An optimistic attitude and the action it encourages seem to spread outward with positive ripple effects. When Nirvan Mullick posted his film about Caine's Arcade on YouTube, he hoped to raise money to provide for a scholarship for Caine. His original goal was $25,000. Less than a year later, the fund was nearing $250,000.

As donations poured in, Mullick decided to expand his vision and create the Imagination Foundation. The goal of this charitable organization is to find children like Caine and to encourage and provide funds for their creative activities. After seeing the Caine's Arcade film, young people around the world began sending in video examples of their own cardboard inventions.

The Imagination Foundation organized a Global Cardboard Challenge a year after the arcade became famous. Teachers began showing the film about Caine in their classrooms, and an international educational program has been launched to encourage students to use their imaginations and build with cardboard.

IF LIFE GIVES YOU LEMONS, MAKE LEMONADE!

An optimistic attitude helps people dream big. Many young people set up lemonade stands to raise a little personal spending money. Other lemonade stands are built in order to change the world. A strong spirit of optimism inspired two children to use lemonade stands for important causes.

Alex's Lemonade Stand Foundation was started by young cancer patient Alexandra Scott. Diagnosed with cancer before her first birthday, Alex was not expected ever to walk. Yet, eventually, she did walk. At age four, when her cancer was in remission, Alex decided to raise money to help other young patients by selling lemonade. The first lemonade stand raised $2,000, and Alex's family put up a stand each year to continue raising funds for cancer research.

Alex died at age eight, but she knew that she had helped raise over $1 million to fund research that will

Cancer patient Alexandra Scott died young, but not before raising thousands of dollars to help others like herself. Alex's Lemonade Stand Foundation continues in her honor and has raised millions of dollars for cancer research since 2000.

benefit others with her disease. Her parents established a foundation in her honor and have raised over $55 million since 2000. The Alex's Lemonade Stand Foundation believes "every person can make a difference in the world."

At age eight, Vivienne Harr believed that her efforts could help bring an end to human slavery around the world. Her lemonade stand has since raised thousands of dollars and brought the issue greater public attention.

Vivienne Harr, an eight-year-old in California has set up a lemonade stand and plans to continue operating it until she has raised $150,000 to give to an organization working to end human slavery. Will she reach her goal? Her story is spreading worldwide through radio and the Internet. Her online video challenges viewers "to be one person who helps." Inspired by a photo of two children in Nepal engaged in forced hard labor, Vivienne believed her efforts could make a difference.

Harr is one of many, many young Americans leading comparatively comfortable lives who feel obligated to pass along their good fortune to others. These young people are optimistic about improving the lives of those who are less fortunate or who are living in challeng-ing circumstances. Their commitment to harness their optimism to positive and direct action that achieves concrete results shows the transformative power of this character strength.

GLOSSARY

ANXIETY A feeling of worry, nervousness, or unease.

CHARACTER The attributes or features that make up and distinguish an individual.

CHARACTER TRAIT A personality quality that determines, distinguishes, or defines the way a person acts or thinks. A number of character traits make up who someone is.

CONSEQUENCE The result or effect of an action or condition.

DEPRESSION A mental condition in which a person remains very unhappy, without energy or interest in normal activities, over a long period of time.

DISPUTE To question whether an idea or supposed fact is actually true.

DISTRACT To take one's attention or focus off of something.

EXPLANATORY STYLE The way in which a person mentally explains why events in his or her life happen as they do.

GRATITUDE Thankfulness.

MAGNETIC RESONANCE SCANNER A medical machine that produces images of the brain and other internal organs.

NEUROSCIENTIST Someone who specializes in the study of the brain and nervous system.

OPTIMISM A way and habit of thinking in which someone expects most situations to turn out well.

OUTCOME The way something turns out; the consequence of an action or series of actions.

PESSIMISM The opposite of optimism. A habitual expectation that the worst thing will happen or a tendency to primarily see the negative side of situations.

POSITIVE EDUCATION A movement in the field of education that focuses on promoting happiness and well-being.

PROACTIVE Dealing with a situation by causing a desired effect to occur rather than waiting to react to the situation and its outcome or consequences.

PSYCHOLOGIST A scientist who studies the human mind, especially how the mind affects behavior.

REMISSION A lessening of the seriousness of a disease; a temporary recovery.

SELF-FULFILLING PROPHECY Something that happens largely because one expected it to happen.

STRESS Mental, physical, or emotional pressure.

BAM! (Body and Mind)
Centers for Disease Control and Prevention (CDC)
1600 Clifton Road
Atlanta, GA 30333
(404) 639-3311
Web site: http://www.bam.gov
BAM! offers information and support about diseases, fitness, peer pressure, nutrition, and other topics relevant to developing happiness, resilience, and emotional and physical health.

Canadian Children's Optimist Foundation
5205 Boulevard Métropolitain Est, Bureau 200
Montréal, QC H1R 1Z7
Canada
(514) 593-440l, ext. 336
Web site: http://www.optimistcanada.org
This organization is related to Optimist International. It provides assistance and educational opportunities for boys and girls involved in Optimist programs in Canada.

Canadian Positive Psychology Association (CPPA)
c/o Department of Business
University of Guelph
50 Stone Road East

Guelph, ON N1G 2W1
Canada
(519) 824-4120
Web site: http://www.positivepsychologycanada.com
The CPPA aims to improve the mental health of Canadians
by sharing information among psychologists and other
health professionals and by promoting positive psychology through publications, through seminars, and
over the Internet.

Character Education Partnership
1025 Connecticut Avenue NW, Suite 1011
Washington, DC 20036
(202) 296-7743
Web site: http://www.character.org
This nonprofit umbrella organization aims to promote
character education in schools. It provides resources
and training for teachers to help them teach character traits (like optimism) along with academic
subjects.

International Positive Psychology Association (IPPA)
19 Mantua Road
Mount Royal, NJ 08061
(856) 423-2862
Web site: http://www.ippanetwork.org

The IPPA works to promote positive psychology by encouraging cooperation and communication among researchers, teachers, students, and practitioners of positive psychology.

Office of Adolescent Health
U.S. Department of Health and Human Services
c/o Office of the Assistant Secretary for Health
1101 Wootton Parkway, Suite 700
Rockville, MD 20852
(240) 453-2846
Web site: http://www.hhs.gov/ash/oah
This government office provides publications and links to resources that promote physical and mental health for young people.

Optimist International
4494 Lindell Boulevard
St. Louis, MO 63108
(800) 500-8130
Web site: http://optimist.org
Optimist International is an association of more than 2,900 Optimist Clubs around the world dedicated to "bringing out the best in kids." These local clubs carry out service projects and provide scholarships to help young people. Junior Optimist Octagon International

(JOOI) involves young people as volunteers in service projects.

WEB SITES

Due to the changing nature of Internet links, Rosen Publishing has developed an online list of Web sites related to the subject of this book. This site is updated regularly. Please use this link to access the list:

http://www.rosenlinks.com/7CHAR/Opti

FOR FURTHER READING

Anchor, Shawn. *The Happiness Advantage: The Seven Principles of Positive Psychology That Fuel Success and Performance at Work*. New York, NY: Crown Publishing, 2010.

Auderset, Marie-José. *Walking Tall: How to Build Confidence and Be the Best You Can Be.* New York, NY: Amulet/Harry N. Abrams, 2008.

Duhigg, Charles. *The Power of Habit: Why We Do What We Do in Life and Business*. New York, NY: Random House, 2012.

Fox, Marci, and Leslie Sokol. *Think Confident, Be Confident for Teens: A Cognitive Therapy Guide to Overcoming Self-Doubt and Creating Unshakable Self-Esteem.* Oakland, CA: New Harbinger Publications, 2011.

Furgang, Adam, and Kathy Furgang. *Cultivating Positive Peer Groups and Friendships* (Middle School Survival Handbook). New York, NY: Rosen Central, 2012.

Hipp, Earl. *Fighting Invisible Tigers: Stress Management for Teens*. Minneapolis, MN: Free Spirit Publishing, 2008.

Johnson, Addie. *Lemons to Lemonade: Little Ways to Sweeten Up Life's Sour Moments.* San Francisco, CA: Conari Press/Red Wheel/Weiser, 2010.

Johnson, Addie. *Life Is Sweet: 333 Ways to Look on the Bright Side and Find the Happiness in Front of

You. San Francisco, CA: Conari Press/Red Wheel/ Weiser, 2008.

Jones, Jami B. *Bouncing Back: Dealing with the Stuff Life Throws at You*. New York, NY: Franklin Watts/ Scholastic, 2007.

Lucas, Eileen. *More Than the Blues? Understanding and Dealing with Depression.* Berkeley Heights, NJ: Enslow Publishers, 2009.

Lyubomirsky, Sonja. *The How of Happiness: A New Approach to Getting the Life You Want*. New York, NY: Penguin Press, 2007.

Orr, Tamra. *Beautiful Me: Finding Personal Strength and Self-Acceptance*. Edina, MN: ABDO Publishing, 2009.

Quick, Matthew. *Sorta Like a Rock Star.* New York, NY: Little, Brown and Company, 2010.

Schab, Lisa M. *The Anxiety Workbook for Teens: Activities to Help You Deal with Anxiety and Worry.* Oakland, CA: New Harbinger Publications, 2008.

Seligman, Martin. *Flourish: A Visionary New Understanding of Happiness and Well-Being.* New York, NY: Free Press, 2012.

Seligman, Martin. *Learned Optimism: How to Change Your Mind and Your Life*. New York, NY: Vintage, 2006.

Simons, Rae. *Survival Skills: How to Handle Life's Catastrophes*. Broomall, PA: Mason Crest Publishers, 2009.

Smith, Ian K. *Happy: Simple Steps to Get the Most Out of Life*. New York, NY: St. Martin's Press, 2010.

Walker, Robert. *Live It: Optimism*. New York, NY: Crabtree Publishing, 2009.

Zucker, Faye, and Joan E. Huebl. *Beating Depression: Teens Find Light at the End of the Tunnel*. New York, NY: Franklin Watts, 2007.

BIBLIOGRAPHY

Brody, Jane E. "A Richer Life by Seeing the Glass Half Full." *New York Times*, May 22, 2012. Retrieved September 2012 (http://well.blogs.nytimes.com/2012 /05/21/a-richer-life-by-seeing-the-glass-half-full).

Carnegie, Dale. *How to Stop Worrying and Start Living.* New York, NY: Gallery Books, 2004.

CNN PressRoom. "Fierce Five Celebrate Victory." August 16, 2012. Retrieved November 2012 (http:// cnnpressroom.blogs.cnn.com/2012/08/16 /fierce-five-gymnasts-talk-olympics-victory-with -soledad-obrien).

Covey, Stephen R. *The 7 Habits of Highly Successful People.* New York, NY: Free Press, 2004.

Davis, Katie. "Jesse's Story: An Urban Teen Beats the Odds." NPR.org, August 22, 2008. Retrieved October 2012 (http://www.npr.org/templates/story /story.php?storyId=93850513).

Duffy, John. *The Available Parent: Radical Optimism for Raising Teens and Tweens*. Berkeley, CA: Viva Editions, 2011.

Ehrenreich, Barbara. *Bright-Sided: How the Relentless Promotion of Positive Thinking Has Undermined America*. New York, NY: Metropolitan Books/Henry Holt and Company, 2009.

Fox, Elaine. *Rainy Brain, Sunny Brain: How to Retrain Your Brain to Overcome Pessimism and Achieve a More Positive Outlook.* New York, NY: Basic Books, 2012.

Frontline. "Drop Out Nation." PBS.org, September 25, 2012. Retrieved October 2012 (http://video.pbs.org /video/2283603203).

Isaacson, Andy. "The Perfect Moment Goes Perfectly Viral." *New Yorker*, April 24, 2012. Retrieved September 2012 (http://www.newyorker.com/online/blogs/culture /2012/04/caines-arcade-nirvan-mullick.html).

Kuo, Vivian. "From Scrubbing Floors to Ivy League: Homeless Student to Go to Dream College." CNN .com, June 8, 2012. Retrieved June 22, 2012 (http:// www.cnn.com/2012/06/07/us/from-janitor-to -harvard/index.html).

Patterson, Kerry, et al. *Change Anything: The New Science of Personal Success*. New York, NY: Business Plus, 2011.

Peale, Norman Vincent. *The Power of Positive Thinking*. New York, NY: Ishi Press, 2011.

Pfeiffer, Eric. "Eight-Year-Old's Lemonade Stand Helps Combat Human Slavery." Yahoo!News, August 15, 2012. Retrieved November 2012 (http://news.yahoo .com/blogs/sideshow/8-old-girl-raising-150k -combat-human-slavery-185900395.html).

Scioli, Anthony, and Henry Biller. *The Power of Hope: Overcoming Your Most Daunting Life Difficulties— No Matter What*. Deerfield Beach, FL: Health Communications, Inc., 2010.

Segerstrom, Suzanne C. *Breaking Murphy's Law: How Optimists Get What They Want from Life— and Pessimists Can Too.* New York, NY: Guilford Publications, 2006.

Seligman, Martin, and Christopher Peterson. *Character Strengths and Virtues: A Handbook and Classification.* New York, NY: Oxford University Press, 2004.

Sharot, Tali. *The Optimism Bias: A Tour of the Irrationally Positive Brain.* New York, NY: Pantheon Books, 2011.

Tough, Paul. *How Children Succeed: Grit, Curiosity, and the Hidden Power of Character.* Boston, MA: Houghton Mifflin Harcourt, 2012.

Tough, Paul. *Whatever It Takes: Geoffrey Canada's Quest to Change Harlem and America.* New York, NY: Mariner Books, 2009.

Tough, Paul. "What If the Secret to Success Is Failure?" *New York Times Magazine*, September 18, 2011. Retrieved June 2012 (http://www.nytimes.com/2011/09/18/magazine/what-if-the-secret-to-success-is-failure.html?pagewanted=all&_r=0).

INDEX

ABOUT THE AUTHOR

Writer and educator Terry Teague Meyer lives in Houston, Texas. She writes both nonfiction and poetry. She has long considered herself an optimist.

PHOTO CREDITS